# the Tenacious Flower

# THE TENACIOUS FLOWER

Published by Emily Poletick Job 2022

All inquiries should be directed to
emilypjob@gmail.com

Visit our website at: www.emilypjob.wixsite.com/tenaciousflower

First Edition: October 2022

Hardcover ISBN: 979-8-218-02721-6
eBook ISBN: 979-8-218-06132-6

*Dedicated to my dearest Matt
and our darlings Sydney and Wyatt*

# Thank You

To those I trusted to help me get the words just right: Matt Job, Richard Poletick, Jerrica Mah, Melissa Sheldon, Jan Horton

To Penny Weber who magically turned the manuscript into gorgeous illustrations
**www.PennyWeberIllustrations.com**

To Michelle Manley for effortless friendship and professional formatting
**www.GraphiqueDesignCo.com**

To Leanne Tangney photography for saving me from my selfie

To my cheerleaders who pushed me forward and gave me courage:
Marcy Poletick, Jackie Leonetti, Mary Pendleton, Randy Compean

To my angels who trusted my vision with financial support: Dana Aboissiere, Sarah Ahern, Gabriel Alvarez, Stephanie Barbre, Meghann Barloewen, Bina Barth, Elise Blalock, Melissa Pudiwitr Blanton, Jennifer Boylan, Lindsay Braverman,* Alicia Brown, Patricia Cameron, Angela Carpio,† Erin Clark,* Amanda Crews, Susan Cox,* Chelsea Cruzan, Leanne Daniels,* Megan Daugherty, Leah Davis & Peyton, Allison DeMark, Jill Devlin,* Tammy Dixon, Amanda Duff,* Steven Eastman,* Kimberlee Evelo, Mary Flander, Renee Gillespie,* Rachel Glaze, Nancy Green, Marcie Hawkins, Joan Herrick, Krista Jane, Misty Janssen,* Doreen Job, Shannon Job, Teresa Johnson, Pushpinder Kaur, Gayane Keshishian, Gloria Kim, Mary Krueger-Hilliard,* Yvonne Lane, Jackie Leonetti,* Crystal Lincoln, Tony Lugo, Patrice Madrid, Molly Mahoney,* Aaliyah McLaughlin, David McClellan, Sandy McDowell, Shayda Mecca, Glenn Miller, Stephanie Miller, Susanna Melvin, Paige Montanio,* † Kim Eastman Mora,* Maggie Mora, Patrick M. Murphy,* Stacey Newman, Elizabeth Parker, Dottie Pendleton, Mary Pendleton, Nicole Pierce, Tess Pignataro, Karrie Pittman, Ruschka Sanguinetti, Drew Scallan, Stephanie Schrader, Kim Stoot, Lynn Strohmenger, Julie Taylor,* Theresa Traska, Kelly Triggs, Linda VanderHyde, Michelle Ventigan, Jasmin Willerer, Jennifer Willoughby, Angie Wintheiser, Chuck & Sandy Zelle

*generously donated a book to local schools or children's hospitals
†kidney transplant recipients and real life tenacious flowers

*For my Godchildren: Kieran, Sloane and MaKenna*

One Spring morning, when the earth was waking from its long seasonal slumber, a small stem emerged from a pair of bristled leafs that rested on the ground.

It didn't take long for the little bud to begin to bloom. As she opened her eyes for the first time, she discovered her home was in the middle of a vast perfectly manicured lawn.

Bella was excited to see the sun rising over her backyard, and having grown very tired of being cooped up in the house all winter, she swung the backdoor open wide and ran outside.

Bella was about 20 steps into her great escape when she looked down and quickly discovered a new friend. "Dandy Lion!" she shouted with glee. "How very nice to meet you!"

The small budding flower looked up and, to her delight, she
had not been trampled by Bella's huge and intrusive feet!

Bella laid down on the damp grass, cupped the tiny flower
in her hands and whispered, "You are the most wonderful
thing I have ever seen!"

Then, like a bolt of lightning, Bella ran off.

Dandy Lion straightened herself up a little. The warm sun felt glorious on her face. Just as she was beginning to settle in...there came a horrible noise, like thunder.

It was slowly approaching, and Dandy Lion could see a very large person pushing something in her direction.

It looked like a **MONSTeR!**

Bella came back into sight. She was flailing her arms and yelling, "Daddy, Daddy! NO! You will run over my new friend!"

Bella's father quickly turned off the lawn mower and searched for something or someone that his daughter may have been referring to. Scratching his head, he said with a hint of irritation in his voice, "Bella, all I see is this weed!"

Bella looked at her dad with frustration and confusion,

"Daddy! I do not see any weeds. Just this happy yellow flower!"

With patience and understanding, Bella's father assured her he would not bother the dandelion.

Dandy Lion soon found out where Bella had gone,
for the child began introducing the flower to her collection
of plastic fairy figurines and surrounding the flower with
beautiful rocks of various shapes, sizes and textures.

After Bella spent hours entertaining Dandy Lion, she heard her mother call from the porch, "Lunch is ready, my Beautiful Flower!"

The sun rose and fell a number of times
before Dandy Lion saw Bella again.

On this day the young girl was delighted to show Dandy Lion the family's pet, who had recently woken from her reptilian hibernation.

"Look, Dandy Lion! I want to introduce you to Zuri, which is short for Maua Mazuri. She is my pet tortoise! Her name means 'beautiful flower' in Swahili."

Bella gently set her companion down and opened a book
she had brought to read to her flora and fauna.

"Oh my!," yelped Bella. "That is no way to make friends,
Zuri! We do NOT bite others whom we have just met!"

Dandy Lion felt great relief when her guests had departed after their afternoon gathering. She felt a twinge of sadness come over her, however, when something deep within her being told her that this stage of her life cycle was soon coming to an end. Dandy Lion wanted to give Bella a gift to thank her for the most perfect patch of grass; a place of joy and comfort. She closed up tight and got to work.

Day dawned. As the sun began to dry the dew, Bella came to visit her flower friend and let out a cry so alarming that her mother came rushing to her side.

"Why are you so sad, my Bella-bina?" Bella whimpered as her mother gently plucked the dandelion from its leaves. "Dandy Lion has given you a wish," her mother whispered reassuringly. She handed her child the pappus puff. "Follow me."

Bella stared at her feet; her throat felt tight making words impossible to speak. She took her mom's hand as they walked a short distance. When Bella had mustered enough courage to raise her gaze, she saw that they were at the park across from her home. Bella's mother leaned down to speak softly into her daughter's ear, "Make a wish, Bella. Now blow."

Bella squeezed her eyes tight and thought about becoming a veterinarian when she grew up...she thought about the realistic doll she wished for on her birthday... she thought about baking cookies with her Grandma whom she was hoping might come for a visit soon. Then she exhaled.

"I want a million more wishes,"
and let out a puff of air.

That evening after getting ready for bed, Bella's mother asked her to think about all the good things she hoped for. She asked her to imagine each of those things as little dandelion seeds floating in the air, looking for just the right spot to end their flight and settle in to start growing.

"Now is the time…" mom said in a hushed
tone as she entered Bella's bedroom to help
her little one get dressed for the day.

"I have a surprise to show you." She pulled the soft drapery aside and motioned for Bella to join her at the window. She pointed to the grassy field where Bella had stood a few short weeks before. This time it was dotted with dozens of happy yellow flowers.

"See, Bella! Your wish came true! There are a million more wishes growing ...

You, my child, with the help of a dandelion, have given us all a million more opportunities to spread our own hopes and dreams as far as the wind can carry them."

Bella squeezed her stuffy a little tighter. Her heart
was a little lighter and her smile was a whole lot brighter.

CPSIA information can be obtained
at www.ICGtesting.com
Printed in the USA
LVHW071559190223
739890LV00007B/94